PEACHTREE

To Katherine

Gary and Ray copyright © Frances Lincoln Limited 2009
Text and illustrations copyright © Sarah Adams 2009

First published in Great Britain in 2009 and in the USA in 2010 by
Frances Lincoln Children's Books, 4 Torriano Mews,
Torriano Avenue, London NW5 2RZ

www.franceslincoln.com

British Library Cataloguing in Publication Data available on request

ISBN: 978-1-84507-955-0

The illustrations in this book are lino prints

Printed in China

1 3 5 7 9 8 6 4 2

Gary and Ray

Sarah Adams

F

FRANCES LINCOLN
CHILDREN'S BOOKS

Deep in an African forest there lived
a gorilla called Gary.

All the other animals had friends to play with.
But Gary was sad because he was all alone.

The elephants played together.

The monkeys hugged each other.

Even the owls were friends.

But poor Gary had no one. The children from
the nearby village were too afraid to come near.
If only Gary could tell them that he was frightened too.

At night he dreamed that fierce hunters came to take him away. But no one was there to comfort him when he woke up.

"Will anyone ever love me?" thought Gary.

Suddenly to Gary's surprise a tiny sunbird
flew into his hand.

"Aren't you scared of me?" asked Gary.

"No," answered the bird. "You looked
so unhappy, I came to say hello.
My name is Ray."

Gary and Ray were soon best friends.
They liked to dance…

Sing and

SWING!

Hide-and-seek was their favourite game.

First Ray would hide…

and then Gary.

Ray introduced Gary to his family.
Gary liked to watch them together
but he wished he could have a family
of his own.

Early one morning Gary woke up
to find Ray had gone.
Gary felt lonelier than ever.
He missed his little friend.

Long days passed. Then one morning Gary heard a familiar friendly sound. It was Ray!

"Come with me!" chirped Ray excitedly.

"Where are we going?" asked Gary, overjoyed to see his friend again.

"It's a surprise," said Ray.

For two days, Ray led Gary
deeper into the forest.
Then Gary stopped
in amazement.

"Gary, meet Susan,"
said Ray smiling.

Gary's heart was suddenly filled
with love and hope.
Susan gave a shy smile.
She loved Gary too.

And Gary was never lonely again.

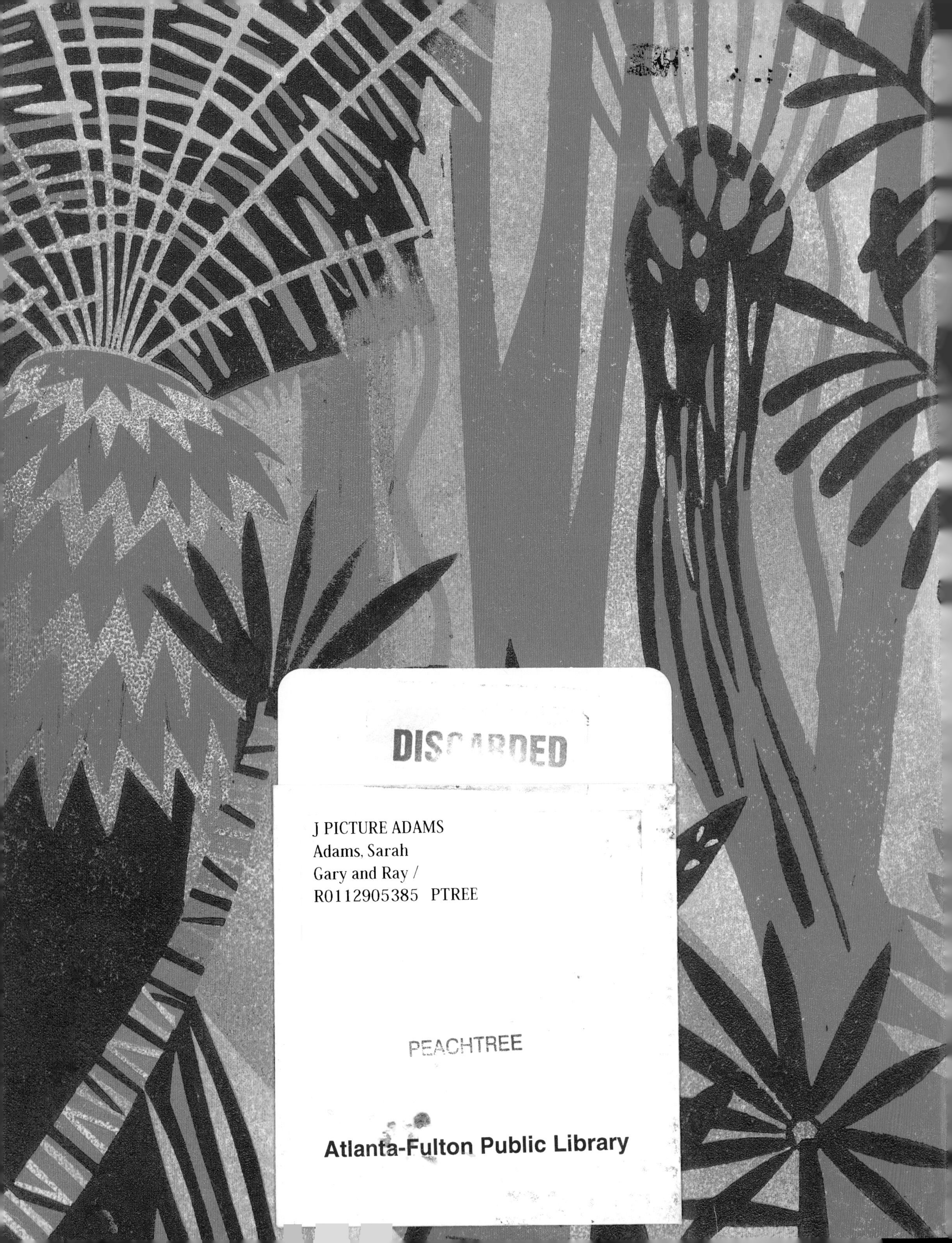